Chaucer's World

We don't know exactly when Geoffrey Chaucer was born, only that it was a few years before the great plague, the Black Death, which struck Europe in 1347 and killed one person in every three. Perhaps it's scarcely surprising that Chaucer used the plague as a background to *The Pardoner's Tale.*

In the Middle Ages, England, like the rest of Europe, was governed by the king and noble families. As a young man, Chaucer fought in France, where he was captured and held to ransom. Luckily he had important friends, including King Edward III, who paid for his release. When Chaucer returned to England he worked for the king in a variety of roles. One job was to be in charge of the building works in the royal palaces. Already well known as a writer, Chaucer finally gave up his work for the king to spend more time writing.

After the Norman Conquest all the important people in England had to speak French, so little poetry was written in English. During Chaucer's lifetime, this began to change. As well as his poems, some stories about King Arthur were written at this time.

The Church was very powerful in the Middle Ages, setting out the rules by which everyone lived their lives. Sometimes this meant that the Church opposed the king. In 1170, archbishop Thomas à Becket had been killed in Canterbury Cathedral by some of the king's knights. Canterbury became a place where pilgrims went, to pray for cures to illnesses. There were a lot of greedy people in the Church who were only interested in money. Among the worst of these were pardoners, who were allowed to forgive people's sins if they gave money to the Church. Pardoners often kept some of this money.

Chaucer seems to have been very unhappy about such corruption. The storytellers in Chaucer's *Canterbury Tales* are pilgrims, but they are not all good people. There is a proud monk and a bad friar, but worst of all is the Pardoner.

Chaucer's Pardoner is particularly nasty, and when he tells his tale, he starts by admitting that he makes a good living by selling fake treasures. No one knows why he did this – perhaps he wanted to show off to his fellow pilgrims how clever he was!

The Classic Collection

Geoffrey Chaucer's
The Pardoner's Tale

Retold by Jan Dean
Illustrated by Chris Mould

HODDER
Wayland

an imprint of Hodder Children's Books

An artist's impression of Geoffrey Chaucer,
1340?–1400.

Telling The Tales

It was spring. The trees were bursting into new, green life. Hedges were full of fluttering birds, singing as they built their nests. After the frozen winter, the world seemed suddenly alive again and all this buzzing energy made people restless. In those days, spring was the time for journeys to famous holy places.

And so a group of travellers met in Southwark at the Tabard Inn. Like hundreds of others, they were setting out upon a holy journey – a pilgrimage to Canterbury.

"Welcome!" the landlord of the Tabard said. "Supper is ready and the wine is poured."

The pilgrims took their places at the table and settled down to eat.

The landlord smiled. He was a big, jolly man and liked to see his customers enjoy themselves.

The pilgrims were people from all walks of life. The landlord grinned as he watched a brave crusader knight share bread and chicken with a lowly cook. It was truly amazing how a pilgrimage brought such people together.

"Now there's a sight you don't see every day!" the landlord muttered, as two nuns sat down beside a ship's captain – who was known to have made his fortune as a pirate!

Suddenly the landlord had an idea. "Ladies and gentlemen!" he cried. "Canterbury is five days' ride from here – and it can be a very dull journey. Why not pass the time by telling stories on the way? The best storyteller will win a dinner – paid for by the rest of us."

There was a moment's silence as the pilgrims listened to the landlord, then a buzz as they reacted to his bright idea.

"*Storytelling?* That's not a bad suggestion…" the lawyer said to the miller.

"Oh, there's nothing I like more than a good story," the rich widow said to the poor ploughman.

"But who will choose the winner?" the Pardoner asked.

"I will," declared the landlord. "I like you all so much I'm going to come with you!"

And so it was decided.

The Pardoner

The Pardoner sang as he rode along.

The landlord sneaked a sideways look at him. He was a strange-looking man. The Pardoner's face was smooth and shiny. His greasy, yellow hair hung in thin ropes over his shoulders. But still he wore the latest style of cloak and hat.

The landlord didn't trust the Pardoner. He was supposed to be a holy man, but he was clearly a crook. He had a saddle-bag full of holy treasures – and every one of them was a fake! He had a tattered pillow slip that he said was the Virgin Mary's veil. Then there were pig's bones that he claimed were the knuckle bones of a saint. And he swore that he had a piece of the sail from St Peter's boat, but it was just a scrap of dirty canvas.

"Buy these holy things," the Pardoner promised, "and you'll be sure to go to heaven!"
What a liar!

But people often fell for his tricks. When the Pardoner travelled to lonely villages in the countryside he preached in the church, then he spoke about the wonderful holy treasures he had.

The people there believed him. He would stare at them with his bulgy eyes, then take his *treasures* from his saddle-bag. Holding them as tenderly as precious silks or finest crystal, he'd weave a web of lies. Like a cunning spider,

the Pardoner would draw his listeners in until they were caught fast by his story. Then they'd buy his false treasures and make him rich.

The Pardoner had listened as the other pilgrims told their stories. He'd do well in the competition – he was sure of it. After all, he made his living by talking people out of their hard-earned money!

At last it was the Pardoner's turn to tell a tale…

"Ladies and gentlemen," he began. "I am a wonderful preacher. First I impress my listeners with a list of famous places I have visited and famous people that I know. Then I speak a few words of Latin – no one understands it, of course – but it sounds convincing! Next I show them my glass cases crammed with worthless rags and old bones and I pretend that they are marvellous relics!

"'Look,' I say, 'this is the shoulder bone of one of Jacob's sheep – that's Jacob, grandson of Abraham in the Bible. This shoulder bone has magical powers. It can cure diseases of all kinds…'

"Then I tell them, 'This glove is magic, too.
Whoever puts his hand in it will have a
marvellous crop of wheat or oats. The farmer
who wears this glove will harvest far more than
he planted! That is, providing he makes a
generous payment for the glove.' *Generous
payments,* that's what I'm after and so I always
preach my sermon on the same theme –
GREED. *The love of money is the root of all evil –*
it's the subject of every sermon that I preach.

So everyone who listens is keen to show that they don't value wealth more than they value a holy life. To prove that they don't care for money, they give lots of it away in the collection plate.

"Now, good pilgrims, I will tell you my tale. It's the very same tale I tell in sermons to show how love of money kills the soul…"

The Pardoner's Story

Once, there was a gang of youths who were the terror of the neighbourhood. They ran riot – drinking, gambling, dancing and swearing – all night long. This story is about three of these boys – let's call them Long Tom, Fast Jack and Nick the Red.

One afternoon, the three youths sat drinking in the tavern, when they heard a sound – *Tink. Tink. Tink.*

"Is that a bell?" Jack asked.

Tom was sprawled across the bench. "Might be. Go and see," he mumbled.

"I can't be bothered," Jack said. "You go, Nick."

Nick pushed his red hair out of his eyes and yawned.

"Hey! Serving boy!" Nick called rudely. "Look out of the window and find out what that noise is all about."

"No need," the boy answered. "I know what it is. It's a funeral bell. They're taking a body to the graveyard."

Tom sat up in a rush, sending his pint of beer flying. "Who's dead?" he asked. "Is it anyone we know?"

The serving boy gave a sly grin. "You know him all right. He's one of your gang. This time yesterday you were drinking with him."

Nick blinked nervously. "What happened?" he asked.

"Oh, it was nasty," the serving boy said.
"Your friend was blind drunk – lying on the
bench there – just about where you are now…
and while he snored and grunted in came Death
and stole away his life!"

"What? *Here?*" Nick gulped and glanced down
at the bench where Death had been.

But Tom thumped his fist down on the table.
"*Stole* his life, you say? Then Death's no better
than a thief!"

"That's true," the boy replied, "and since the plague came, Death has stolen thousands. There are farms around here where the corn has gone to seed, and the cattle all run wild, because Death has taken all the farm hands and the farmer, too. Last night he came in here, looked at your friend and speared him through the heart. He took his life, then turned without a word and left."

"I think Death's a villain!" Long Tom shouted. "And if I meet him I shall tell him so."

"We all meet him, sir," the tavern boy said. "There's no avoiding him. But we should be ready when he comes. If we live a good life, there's nothing to fear in Death."

"Death's a rogue, I say," Tom shouted as he staggered to his feet. "He's a killer. And I swear, here and now, I'll search him out! I'll find him and put an end to him! Jack, Nick, you're good fellows – let's make a promise now to track down Death and kill him!"

Fuddled with beer, the other two boys wobbled to their feet and raised their tankards. "Death to Death!" they cried. "We'll drink to that!"

"We'll be blood brothers while we hunt him down," Tom vowed.

Then all three of them burst through the door of the tavern and tumbled out on to the street.

About half a mile from the town they met a wizened old man. "God bless you and keep you safe!" he said.

"Go away, old man," Jack said unkindly. "Don't bother us."

The boys stared at the man's lined face and his gnarled hands. "You're *so* old," Jack said. "Why aren't you dead yet?"

The man gave Jack a hard stare. "I'm cursed," he said. "I cannot die. I wander the earth longing for rest. I want nothing more than to lay down my old bones, but though I may see Death, he will never take me."

"It's a trick!" Nick said. "I think you're Death's spy!" Suddenly he grabbed the old man by the throat and shook him. "Tell me where Death is, or I'll throttle you."

"I'm no spy!" the old man protested. "But I know where Death is. Up this winding road, beyond a green grove, beneath a shady tree, Death sits and waits. Now let me go!"

"Yes!" Tom shouted in triumph. "Now we've got him…"

At once they let the old man go and ran off up the road.

When they reached the green grove, the three
boys slowed down and crept through the trees.

"Can you see him?" Nick asked.

Tom shook his head. But there *was* something
under the distant oak tree… Tom stared.

Something was glittering. *Gold!*

"Treasure!" he yelled.

Forgetting all about their search for Death, the
three of them hurtled across the clearing towards
the shady oak.

"We're rich! *Rich!*" Tom yelled.

"*Millionaires!*" sang Nick.

Jack poured handfuls of coins into his lap in a great golden stream, while Nick's eyes grew round in wonder. "Let's go back to town and start spending some of this," Nick said.

But Tom shook his head. "Wait – let's think about this," he said. "If we suddenly appear with the money, people will think that we've stolen it. So we'll stay here till nightfall. Then we'll carry the gold home under the cover of darkness."

Nick shook his red head. "But it's ages before it gets dark and I'm hungry. And thirsty."

"Me, too," said Jack. "I could eat an ox!"

"All right," Tom said. "Nick and I will stay here and guard the treasure. You go to town and bring us back some food."

"And wine," Nick added. "Don't forget the wine."

"Why me?" Jack said.

"You're the best runner," Nick said. "You're *Fast Jack*, and the youngest, so you'll be the quickest."

"Oh, all right then," Jack said. "If I have to…"

Tom and Nick lay down in the shade of the tree
and gazed at the pile of gold.

"You know what I like best about this treasure?"
Tom asked.

"What?" Nick said.

"There's *lots* of it," Tom sighed happily. "Lots
and lots and lots. Only…"

"Only what?"

"Only, there'd be even more of it if we didn't
have to divide it between three," said Tom.

"What do you mean?" Nick asked suspiciously.

"Why don't we share it between two? You and me. Half each."

"What about Jack?" asked Nick.

"Oh, he's easily dealt with. There are two of us and only one of him. When he comes back we'll ambush him and kill him. Then we'll split the money half and half."

Nick thought about Jack and then looked at the gold. "I'll do it," he said.

In town Jack bought cheese and bread and
sausages and three large bottles of best red wine.
The memory of the treasure glittered in his
mind. He remembered the lovely pile of shiny
gold that lay beneath the tree. But the more he
thought about it, the smaller the pile seemed.
It was far too small a pile to share with Nick and
Tom. So Jack made his way to the chemist's shop.

"Poison?" the chemist asked, staring hard at Jack. "What for?"

"I need to get rid of some pests," Jack said.

The chemist understood at once. "Oh, you've got rats have you? Don't worry, this will do the trick." He handed Jack a packet of white powder.

"Take care," he warned. "This poison is *deadly*. Even one speck of it will kill. Anyone who takes only the tiniest grain of it will die instantly – in *horrible* agony…"

Jack paid for the packet. "It's all right," he said.
"I know what I'm doing."

In a dark alley round the corner from the
shop, Jack set down the three bottles of wine.
Carefully he set his own bottle aside. Then he
opened up the other two. He poured half of
the white powder into the
first bottle and the rest in
the second.

The corks squeaked as Jack re-sealed the bottles. "And Tom and Nick will squeak, too, when they drink this," Jack giggled. "Then they'll be gone and the gold will be all mine."

He glanced at his own bottle. He needed to mark it in some way. It wouldn't do to get it mixed up with the other two! Jack thought for a moment then took out his knife and cut a chunk from the cork. "That should do it," he said cheerfully. "Now I'm safe from harm."

And he sang all the way back to the grove.

"He's coming!" Tom warned when he heard Jack's singing. He and Nick crouched down low in the bushes.

"Nick? Tom? Where are you?" Jack called.

"Here!" Tom roared and out they sprang.

For a second Jack thought it was a joke – mock wrestling like they'd played as children – but then he saw the gleam of Tom's blade and felt the awful stab of Nick's dagger under his ribs.

With a gasp of horror and surprise, Jack lay
dead upon the grass.

Tom and Nick wiped their knives clean. It
was over.

"Fighting's thirsty work," said Nick. "I need
a drink."

"There's plenty here," Tom said, grabbing the
bottles that lay by Jack's body.

"Not that one, it's got a damaged cork," Nick
said. "The other two are fine."

So they opened up the two remaining bottles
and they lay down under the shady tree beside
the winking gold. There they drank each bottle
dry. And as they fell into a drunken sleep Jack's
poison sealed their veins like wax until they, too,
were stiff and cold upon the ground.

Truly these three young men found Death
beneath a shady tree.

After The Tale

So the Pardoner finished off his tale, then looked round at his listeners. "*Greed*, you see," he said. "*Greed* will be the death of you. And sin will kill your body and your soul! You're all sinners – every one… So pay me for a pardon! Now, who'll be first?" The Pardoner turned to the landlord.

"You're the biggest sinner of them all, Landlord. Step forward with your money in your hand and kiss this holy relic – it will save your soul!"

"*You villain!*" shouted the landlord. "You've told us all how you twist money out of people with your tricky stories. Now you're waving that old rag about and saying it's a holy relic. If you ask me it's your holey trousers! Well I'm no fool – you'll get nothing from me."

The Pardoner's bulgy eyes blazed with anger and he was prepared for a fight, but the gracious knight stepped between the two men.

"Calm down," he said. "Shake hands. Make friends. Pardoner, we thank you for your tale. A story on a journey never fails – now, who will tell the next one of our *Canterbury Tales*?